GEORGE O'CONNOR

HERMES

TALES OF THE TRICKSTER

A NEAL PORTER BOOK

:01
First Second
New York

WHILE YOU LIVE—
SHINE, HAVE NO GRIEF AT ALL.
LIFE EXISTS BUT BRIEFLY, AND
TIME DEMANDS AN END...

HO, A STATUE OF LORD HERMES! PROTECTOR OF TRAVELERS!
I SEE YOU ARE SALUTING ME!

I SALUTE YOU TOO, LORD HERMES!
AND IT SEEMS MY COMPANION IS PREPARING TO SALUTE YOU AS WELL, IN HIS OWN WAY.

THOUGH, I IMAGINE YOU WOULD HAVE PREFERRED HE ANOINT YOU WITH OIL...

WELL, THERE'S SOMETHING YOU DON'T SEE EVERY DAY.

LOOK AT THIS, DOG. A SOLITARY COTTAGE, IN THE MIDDLE OF NOWHERE. A SINGLE COW, TIED TO AN OLIVE TREE.

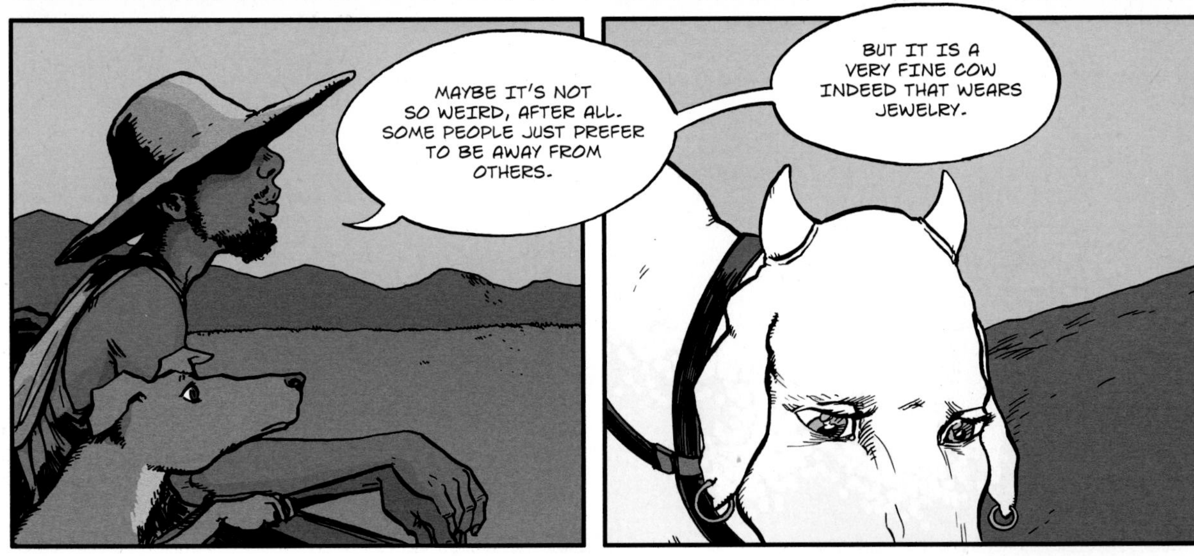
MAYBE IT'S NOT SO WEIRD, AFTER ALL. SOME PEOPLE JUST PREFER TO BE AWAY FROM OTHERS.
BUT IT IS A VERY FINE COW INDEED THAT WEARS JEWELRY.

I DOUBT WE'LL FIND A MORE HOSPITABLE STOP ON OUR ROAD THAN THIS, DOG. I HAD FIGURED WE'D MAKE OUR BED BENEATH THE STARS, BUT WHAT SAY YOU WE TRY TO AVAIL OURSELVES OF THE OWNER OF THIS COTTAGE?
WOOF!

THE DOOR'S OPENING; THEY MUST HAVE SEE—

OH MY!

AREN'T YOU AN EYEFUL!
HEH, I SEE YOU'RE A COMEDIAN...

OOH! NICE ONE!
I'M NO COMEDIAN, BUT MERELY A SIMPLE TRAVELER LOOKING FOR A LITTLE HOSPITALITY.
MIGHT I PROPOSE A BARTER? IN EXCHANGE FOR SOME VICTUALS, A LITTLE WINE, AND A DRY SPOT OF FLOOR FOR MY COMPANION AND ME TO SLEEP ON TONIGHT, I'LL PROVIDE YOU WITH AN EVENING OF ENTERTAINMENT, OF TALES I'VE COLLECTED IN MY JOURNEYS OVER GREAT GREEN GAEA.
I ALWAYS KEEP AN EAR TO THE GROUND FOR A GOOD STORY WHEREVER I GO. HERE'S ONE MY TRAVELING COMPANION HERE TOLD ME HIMSELF.

MANY YEARS AGO, DOGS LIVED A LIFE OF SUBJUGATION TO MANKIND.
THEY LIVED IN SQUALOR AND HAD NO AGENCY OF THEIR OWN. MOST IMPORTANTLY, THEY NEVER GOT ENOUGH FOOD FROM THEIR MASTERS TO SATISFY THEIR HUNGER.
ΠΡΟΣΟΧΗ ΣΚΥΛΟΣ

THE DOGS RAISED THEIR VOICES TO THE HEAVENS AND HOWLED THEIR LAMENT.

PASSING BY ON ONE OF HIS MANY TRAVELS, HERMES HEARD THEIR PRAYERS AND TOOK PITY ON THE DOGS AND THEIR PLIGHT.

HERMES ARRANGED FOR THE DOGS TO HAVE AN AUDIENCE WITH HIS FATHER, ZEUS, KING OF THE GODS, TO PLEAD THEIR CASE.

THE KING OF THE DOGS APPOINTED THREE OF THE FINEST EXAMPLES OF DOGKIND TO SERVE AS THE EMISSARIES TO ZEUS.

THE ARRANGED-FOR TIME ARRIVED, BUT THE DOG AMBASSADORS WERE NOWHERE TO BE FOUND.
SOMEBODY HAS GOT TO INVENT A TIMEPIECE.

FOR THEY, BEING DOGS, HAD LITTLE CONCEPTION OF TIME AND HAD DELAYED TO SATE THEIR HUNGER ON REFUSE.

HERMES FOUND THE MISSING DOG ENVOYS AND ESCORTED THEM TO MOUNT OLYMPUS, HOME OF THE GODS.

THEY WAITED FOR ZEUS TO MAKE HIS APPEARANCE.

WHICH HE DID, THUNDEROUSLY.

OVERCOME WITH AWE, THE DOGS, THEY, WELL...

THEY VOIDED THEIR BOWELS.
ALL OVER MOUNT OLYMPUS.
I DID MENTION THEY HAD BEEN EATING GARBAGE, RIGHT?

ZEUS WAS, UNDERSTANDABLY, LIVID. SILVER-TONGUED HERMES WAS ABLE TO CALM HIM DOWN, AND HE GOT ZEUS TO AGREE TO A SECOND MEETING WITH THE DOGS.
HERMES EXPRESSED HIS DISPLEASURE TO THE KING OF THE DOGS.

THEY WERE BAD, BAD DOGS!

THE KING OF THE DOGS THOUGHT HARD ON HOW TO AVOID A REPEAT OF THE LAST MALODOROUS PERFORMANCE.

A DOG IS A DOG IS A DOG, AFTER ALL, AND A DOG WILL EAT GARBAGE, NO MATTER WHAT.
THE KING OF THE DOGS HAD HIS DOG AMBASSADORS DRINK MANY BOTTLES OF PERFUME IN ADVANCE OF THE MEETING.

THEY ARRIVED EARLY AND WAITED PATIENTLY FOR ZEUS TO RECEIVE THEM.

AS IS HIS WONT, ZEUS MATERIALIZED WITH A CLAP OF THUNDER.

AND THE DOGS, WELL...
AS TRULY AWFUL AS THE SMELL HAD BEEN LAST TIME, IT TURNS OUT THAT WHEN YOU MIX PERFUME WITH POOP, IT BECOMES TRAGICALLY, EXPONENTIALLY, UNBELIEVABLY WORSE.

THE EARTH SHOOK, THE HEAVENS TREMBLED AS ZEUS, KING OF THE GODS, VENTED HIS RAGE.
A GOOD KING DOES NOT PREVENT AMBASSADORS FROM SAFELY LEAVING HIS KINGDOM—

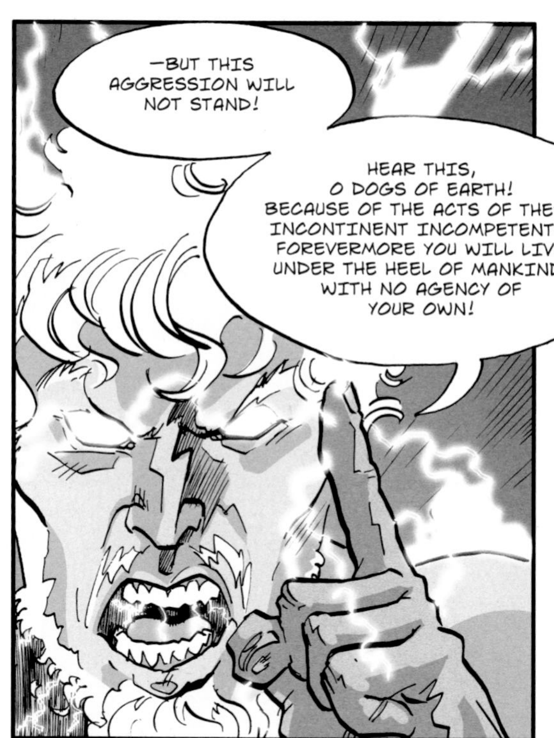
—BUT THIS AGGRESSION WILL NOT STAND!
HEAR THIS, O DOGS OF EARTH! BECAUSE OF THE ACTS OF THESE INCONTINENT INCOMPETENTS, FOREVERMORE YOU WILL LIVE UNDER THE HEEL OF MANKIND, WITH NO AGENCY OF YOUR OWN!

YOU WILL LIVE IN SQUALOR AND NEVER, EVER HAVE ENOUGH FOOD TO SATISFY YOUR APPETITES!!

DOGKIND HEARD ZEUS'S PROCLAMATION AND WERE, TO PUT IT MILDLY, INFURIATED WITH THE AMBASSADORS.

SINCE THEN, DOGS EVERYWHERE HAVE BEEN SEARCHING FOR THE ASININE CANINES WHO COST THEM THEIR ONE SHOT AT A BETTER EXISTENCE.
WHICH IS WHY, TO THIS DAY, WHENEVER TWO DOGS MEET, THEY IMMEDIATELY SNIFF EACH OTHER'S BEHINDS—TO SEE IF THEY SMELL OF PERFUME.

AND THAT'S A SAMPLING OF MY WARES. SO WHAT DO YOU SAY? STORIES FOR HOSPITALITY? DO WE HAVE A DEAL?

HEH. DEAL.

I AM MERELY A WATCHMAN.

I WATCH OVER YONDER COW FOR MY LADY, TO MAKE SURE NO HARM EVER BEFALLS IT.

A NOBLE DEED FOR A NOBLE LADY, EH?

AT ANY RATE, YOUR WINE IS GOOD, AND I THANK YOU FOR IT.

THIS TALK OF COWS AND HERMES PUTS ME IN MIND OF A CERTAIN TALE.

OUR STORY BEGINS ON MOUNT CYLLENE, IN FAR-OFF ARCADIA.

WITH MAIA, THE ELDEST AND BRIGHTEST OF THE PLEIADES.
THE MOST BEAUTIFUL, TOO.

THE PLEIADES ARE THE DAUGHTERS OF THE TITAN ATLAS. MAYBE YOU KNOW HIM?
BIG GUY, KEEPS THE SKY FROM FALLING? ANYWAY, I DIGRESS.

THIS MAIA WAS QUITE THE CATCH, AND IT WASN'T LONG BEFORE SHE CAUGHT THE ATTENTION OF ZEUS, KING OF THE GODS.

NO WOMAN CAN RESIST ZEUS LONG, BUT MAIA WAS ONE SMART GODDESS.

AND SO I MADE SURE YOUR FATHER AND I CONDUCTED OUR LOVE IN SECRET. THERE ARE MANY WHO WOULD WISH US ILL, A CHILD OF THE KING OF THE GODS AND HIS MOTHER.

I HAVE NO DESIRE TO BE HOUNDED LIKE LETO. OR SWALLOWED LIKE METIS.

WHEN YOUR FATHER WAS BORN, RHEA AND GRANDMOTHER EARTH KEPT HIM SAFE FROM KRONOS BY RAISING HIM IN A CAVE.
AND THAT SEEMED TO WORK OUT OKAY FOR HIM, I THINK.

AND THAT'S WHY YOU'LL LIVE HERE WITH ME, IN THIS CAVE.
I WILL KEEP YOU SECRET.
I WILL KEEP YOU SAFE.
MY PERFECT DARLING, HERMES.

THAT NIGHT, THE NEWBORN HERMES SLEPT TIGHT IN HIS MOTHER'S ARMS. MAIA WAS A VERY GOOD MOTHER.

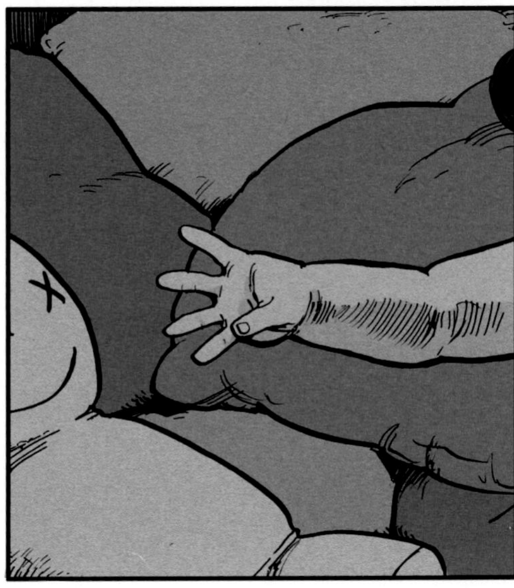

BUT HERMES WAS NOT
A GOOD LITTLE BABY.

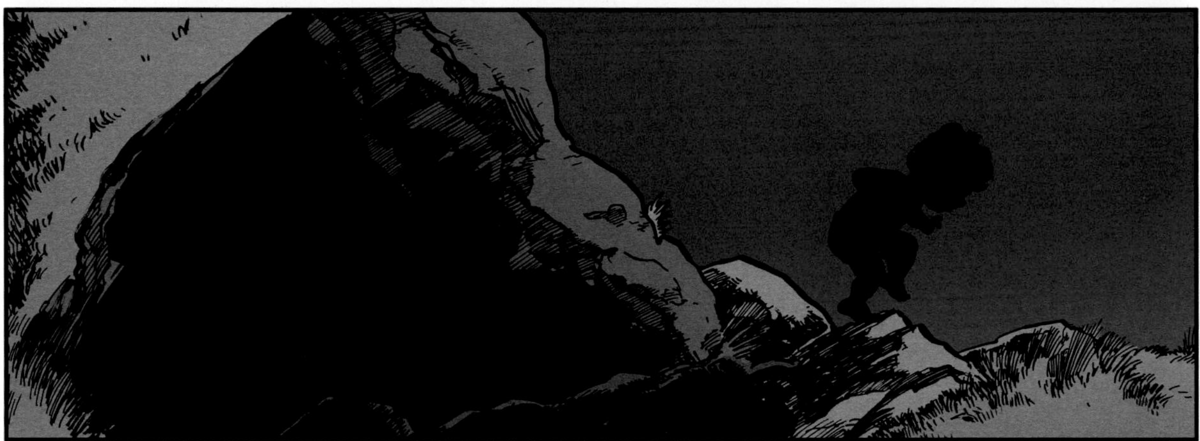

HELLO, WORLD!
WHAT SORT OF TROUBLE CAN WE GET UP TO TONIGHT?

OH,
HELLO THERE,
MR. TORTOISE.

YOU SHOULD
COME INSIDE.
IT'S NOT SAFE FOR
YOU OUT HERE.

NOW
I'M READY.

HAHAHAHAHAHAHAHAHAHAHAHAHAHAHAHA

THE INFANT GODLING FLITTED ALL OVER THE WORLD.

LIKE A THIEF IN THE NIGHT, SEARCHING FOR ADVENTURE.

BUT EVERYONE, EVERYWHERE WAS ASLEEP.

I WONDER, IN THE DAYS BEFORE HERMES, IF PEOPLE DREAMED WHEN THEY SLEPT? WHO BROUGHT THEM THEIR DREAMS IF NOT HERMES?

A SOFT GLOW IN THE DISTANCE CAUGHT YOUNG HERMES'S EYES.

WHAT IS THIS?!

HOLY COWS!!

MOO!
MOO!
MOO, COW, MOO!

OOH! THE BRAND OF APOLLO, MY HALF-BROTHER!
THESE REALLY ARE HOLY COWS!

BOY, *I'D* LIKE SOME COWS!

HEH-HEH...

FIRST,
I'LL
TIE
BARK
TO
YOUR
HOOVES.

THAT WILL DISGUISE YOUR HOOFPRINTS!
BUT WAIT! THERE'S MORE!
I'LL TIE PALM FRONDS TO YOUR TAILS!
AS YOU WALK, THEY WILL SWISH BACK AND FORTH, FURTHER DISRUPTING YOUR TRACKS!

BUT I'M **STILL** NOT DONE!
OKAY, COWS, LISTEN UP!

LOOK INTO MY EYESSS...

MOO.
MOOOO.

NOW...
...WALK **BACKWARD.**

...YES...

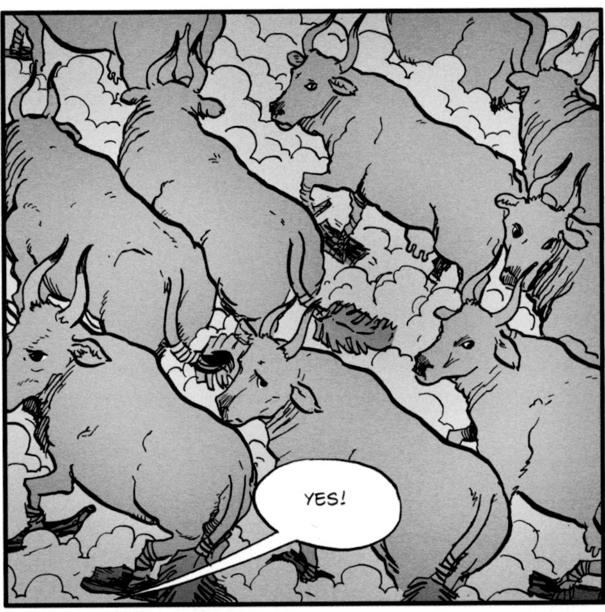
YES!

IT'S WORKING!
THE FINAL TOUCH—
I'LL STRAP GIANT, BACKWARDS FEET TO MY OWN BABY FEET!

BWAHAHAHAHAHA
APOLLO WILL NEVER KNOW WHAT HIT HIM!
GODS, I'M SO **CLEVER**!

THE INFANT HERMES LENT HIS GODLY SPEED TO THE ENSORCELLED HERD, AND THEY TRAVELED A SURPRISING DISTANCE IN THE NIGHT.

THERE WAS NO ONE TO WITNESS THEM PASSING.

ALMOST.

PTUI!

NOTHING TO SEE HERE, OLD MAN!

DAWN APPROACHED, AND HERMES KNIT SOME BRANCHES TOGETHER AND HID APOLLO'S COWS BENEATH.

ALL EXCEPT TWO, WHOM HE SLAUGHTERED.
MOO?

HE DIVIDED THE MEAT INTO TWELVE PORTIONS, WHICH HE BURNED IN SACRIFICE TO THE TWELVE GREAT OLYMPIAN GODS...
COUNTING HIMSELF AS NUMBER TWELVE, OF COURSE.

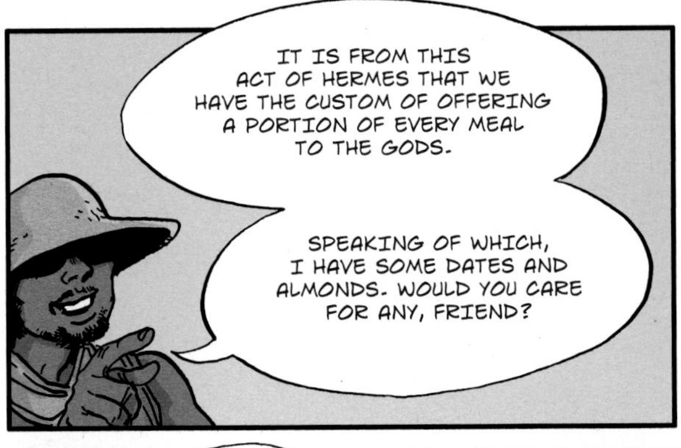
IT IS FROM THIS ACT OF HERMES THAT WE HAVE THE CUSTOM OF OFFERING A PORTION OF EVERY MEAL TO THE GODS.
SPEAKING OF WHICH, I HAVE SOME DATES AND ALMONDS. WOULD YOU CARE FOR ANY, FRIEND?

THANKS.
AND I'LL JUST HELP MYSELF TO SOME MORE OF THIS WINE, HEH-HEH.

LIKE I SAID, A PORTION MUST BE OFFERED TO THE GODS.

HERE IS MY OFFERING— THE DATE PITS AND ALMOND SHELLS! HAH!

GRRR...

DON'T WORRY. I WON'T FORGET YOUR SHARE..

NOW, WHERE WAS I?
GLOMP!

OH YES. HIS NIGHT OF ADVENTURES AT AN END, THE NEWBORN BABE HERMES SNUCK BACK INTO MAIA'S CAVE ON MOUNT CYLLENE.

HERMES!

MOM!
---I MEAN, GOO?
DON'T YOU "GOO" ME! YOU'VE BEEN OUTSIDE ALL NIGHT? WALKING, TALKING? WHAT ELSE ARE YOU HIDING FROM ME?
DIDN'T YOU EVER STOP TO THINK I'D BE WORRIED ABOUT YOU?!?

IN TRUTH, I DID NOT, MOTHER. I AM ONLY A DAY OLD. I AM ONLY JUST LEARNING ABOUT THE WORLD.

OH, HERMES, YOU'RE SO TALENTED, SO PRECOCIOUS, BUT UNDERSTAND—THERE ARE MANY WHO WOULD HURT US FOR WHO YOU ARE. STAY WITH ME, SAFE IN THIS CAVE, UNTIL SUCH TIME AS THE WORLD IS READY FOR YOU.

DON'T WORRY, MOTHER DEAREST. NO ONE BUT YOU AND I WILL EVER KNOW I WAS OUT LAST NIGHT.

SOMEONE STOLE THE SACRED HERD OF APOLLO, LEAVING BEHIND NOTHING BUT—

—DUNG!

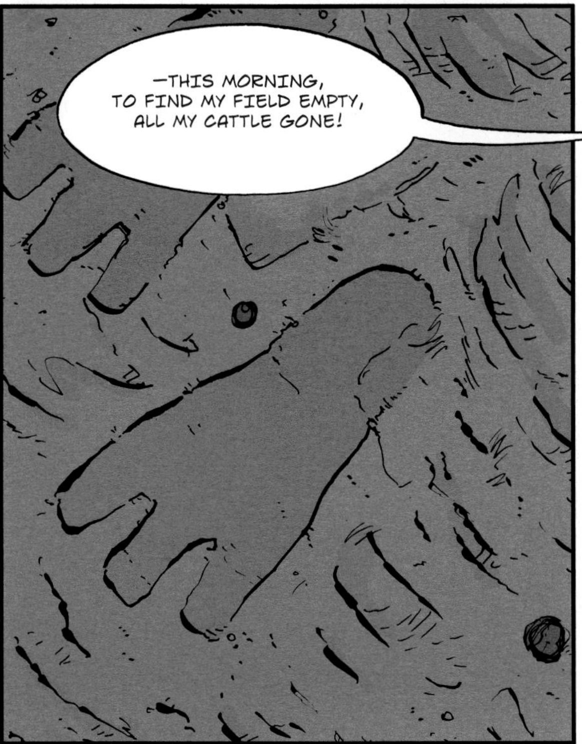
—THIS MORNING, TO FIND MY FIELD EMPTY, ALL MY CATTLE GONE!

I CAN'T MAKE ANY SENSE OF THESE TRACKS, MY SISTER. WHAT DO THEY TELL YOU?
WELL... IT'S HARD TO SAY...

...BUT OFFHAND, IT LOOKS LIKE YOUR COWS WERE STOLEN BY AN INFANT WEARING BACKWARD FALSE FEET, WHO TIED BARK TO THEIR HOOVES, BROOMS TO THEIR TAILS AND SOMEHOW TRAINED THEM TO WALK OUT OF HERE BACKWARD.

WHAT?! THAT'S RIDICULOUS! THANKS FOR NOTHING, ARTEMIS!
YOU ASKED.

THESE TRACKS GO EVERY WHICH WAY! WE CAN'T TELL WHICH WAY THEY WERE HEADED!
WELL, YOUR COWS ARE NOT HERE ANYMORE, SO I'D SAY THEY WENT AWAY...

SOMEONE IS PLAYING APOLLO FOR A FOOL!
SOMEONE IS GOING TO PAY!

APOLLO?
DID YOU ALWAYS HAVE A STATUE OF AN OLD MAN HERE?

WHAT? NO!
THEN MAYBE IT IS MORE THAN IT SEEMS. MAYBE AN OLD MAN SAW MORE THAN HE SHOULD HAVE...

PERHAPS...
FASH!

PTUI!

CHARMING.
SPEAK, OLD MAN! HAVE YOU SEEN ANYTHING UNUSUAL PASS BY HERE?

WELL, I WAS OUT DIGGING FOR MUSHROOMS IN THE EARLY MORNING, AS I DO, WHEN I SAW AN INFANT WEARING BACKWARDS FALSE FEET, WALKING A HERD OF CATTLE BACKWARDS, AND ALL THE CATTLE HAD BARK TIED TO THEIR HOOVES AND BROOMS TO THEIR TAILS.

CALLED IT.
THE INFANT OFFERED ME ONE OF THE COWS IF I KEPT SILENT ABOUT WHAT I HAD SEEN.
BUT THEN A STRANGE-LOOKING MAN CAME BY, WHO SAID HE WAS THE OWNER OF THE COWS.

THAY, MITHTER, I'LL GIVE YOU TWO COWSTH IF YOU TELL ME WHICH WAY THEY WENT.

THEY WENT THATAWAY.
AHA! I KNEW I COULDN'T TRUST YOU!
FASH!

SO YOU WERE RIGHT! BUT WE STILL DON'T KNOW WHO THIS BABY IS OR WHERE MY COWS ARE!
FASH!

WE DON'T KNOW NOW, BUT WE WILL *EVENTUALLY*. YOU'RE THE GOD OF PROPHECY; WHY DON'T YOU LOOK INTO THE FUTURE, TO WHEN YOU DO KNOW?

I, UH, WAIT— DOES THAT EVEN MAKE SENSE?
YOU TELL ME. I HAVE TO GO BACK TO OLYMPUS. HAPPY HUNTING!

AHEM.

GREETINGS, MAIA, DAUGHTER OF ATLAS.

WHO— APOLLO?!
UH-OH...

WHAT ARE YOU DOING HERE, FAR SHOOTER? DID HERA SEND YOU?!
HERA? NOT AT ALL! DO YOU SEE THIS IN MY HANDS?

THIS IS THE GOLDEN CROP I USED TO CORRAL MY SACRED HERD OF FIFTY COWS. A GIFT FROM HEPHAISTOS, IT'S PERFECTLY BALANCED. IMPECCABLY CRAFTED.
I SAY "USED TO" BECAUSE I HAVE NO MORE CATTLE. SOME THIEF MADE AWAY WITH THEM LAST NIGHT.
THIS THIEF, RIGHT HERE!

HERMES?!
WELL, MOM, IT'S LIKE THIS...

I'M THE SON OF ZEUS! YOU AND I, WE DESERVE BETTER THAN THIS CAVE, THIS HIDDEN LIFE!
AND WE GET THAT BY STEALING FROM APOLLO?!
HE ADMITS IT!

IF YOU THINK I WON'T WHIP AN INFANT, LITTLE HALF-BROTHER...
THEN YOU DON'T KNOW APOLLO.
FIRST, YOU ARE GOING TO RETURN MY PROPERT—
ZIP!

FEET DON'T FAIL ME NOW!

—WON'T ESCAPE ME THAT EASILY.
YIKES!

ACKH!
THHPT!

UCK!

TEE-HEE.

RRGGH...

DOGHEADS!

BIG FEET!

?
GRANDPA!

STOP RUNNING—
YOU'RE ONLY MAKING
THIS WORSE FOR
YOURSELF!
HOW SO?

ARE YOU
GOING TO WHIP
ME?
YES!!

THEN THAT
WOULD BE PRETTY
DUMB OF ME TO STOP
RUNNING.
?!

BEHIND
YOU!

COMING
THROUGH!

CAN'T WE TALK ABOUT THIS LIKE CIVILIZED GODS?

ACKPTH! SPUTTER!
GOT YOU NOW, YOU LI—

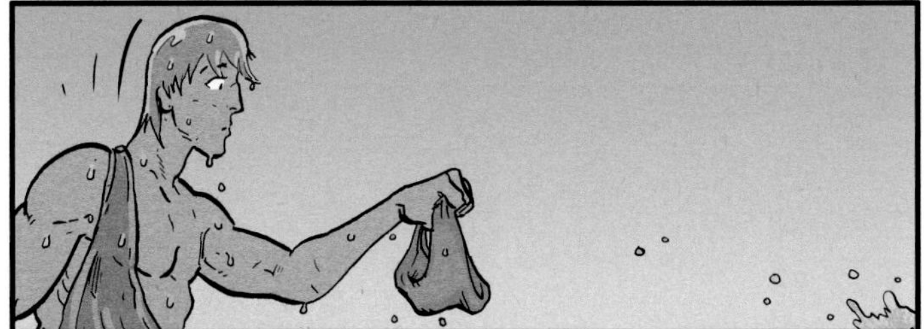

EW.

plip!

DAAAAAAAAAAAAAAAAAAAAA...

-AAAAAAAAAAAAAAAAA-

AAADDY!

"DADDY"?
HA-HA, AH, HMM—

WHERE IS HE?!?!?

WHERE IS THAT MISERABLE, THIEVING, LYING, LITTLE @#&%?!?!
APOLLO! WHAT HAPPENED TO YOU?
HE HAPPENED! THIS MISBEGOTTEN SON OF ZEUS! THIS...HERMES! HE STOLE MY SACRED COWS, THEN LED ME ON A CHASE ALL OVER GRANDMOTHER EARTH!

THIS LITTLE BABY DID THAT?
YES! HE LOOKS INNOCENT, BUT HE'S FILLED WITH TRICKERY! AND LIES! AND HE'S FAST! AND SNEAKY!
HE TIED BARK TO MY COWS' FEET AND MADE THEM WALK BACKWARD! HE TIED BIG FAKE FEET TO HIS FEET! EVEN ARTEMIS COULDN'T TELL WHAT WAS GOING ON!
YES, I COULD.
THESE ARE VERY SERIOUS CHARGES YOUR BROTHER HAS LEVELED AGAINST YOU. DO YOU HAVE ANYTHING TO SAY FOR YOURSELF, LITTLE HERMES?
HE FORGOT TO MENTION I ALSO TIED BROOMS TO THEIR TAILS. I TOTALLY DID THAT, TOO.
OH, HAHA, ZEUS, THIS ONE...
THIS ONE, I LIKE.

AARRRGH!!
YOU'RE ALL LAUGHING... AT HIM! AT ME!

NO ONE IS LAUGHING AT YOU, APOLLO.
I AM.
I CAN VOUCH FOR APOLLO. THIS BABY DID STEAL APOLLO'S CATTLE. HE IS NOT TO BE UNDERESTIMATED.

YOU JUST HOP DOWN HERE, HERMES. THE ADULTS ARE TALKING.
OKAY, POP!

LOOK, I KNOW THIS SEEMS RIDICULOUS! BUT HE IS ONE DAY OLD, AND HE MANAGED TO DO THIS! HE'S TOO DANGEROUS TO RUN FREE!

HI, I'M HERMES. NICE TO MEET YOU.
CHARMED.

TOO DANGEROUS TO RUN FREE? HE IS AN INFANT, APOLLO.

OOH! I LIKE THIS CHAIR! CAN THIS BE MY CHAIR?

NO! THAT'S MY CHAIR! GET OFF IT!

I SHOULD BE ANGRY...
BUT I AM JUST ENJOYING THIS SO MUCH...

HONESTLY, YOU ALL DON'T GET IT!

YOU THINK IT'S SO FUNNY AND CUTE, HIM FLITTING ABOUT EVERYWHERE LIKE THIS, BUT YOU DON'T KNOW HOW INFURIATING HE IS!

WILL YOU BE SO HAPPY WHEN HE BREAKS IN TO YOUR PALACES, STEALS YOUR TREASURES?

plink plink plink

WILL YOU... UH...

UM... WHAT'S THAT YOU'RE PLAYING?

I CALL IT A LYRE.

WHERE DID YOU GET IT?

I JUST MADE IT.

IT SOUNDS... AMAZING.

THANKS!

WANNA TRY IT?

YOU CAN KEEP IT IF YOU WANT.
I...CAN?

WELL, THERE, APOLLO... I'D SAY THAT'S WORTH THE PRICE OF A FEW COWS, WOULDN'T YOU?

NO!
YOU DON'T UNDERSTAND. THOSE WERE COWS! THIS LYRE, IT'S A WORK OF ART!
I MUST GIVE YOU SOMETHING BETTER, SOMETHING GREATER! SOMETHING WORTHY OF YOUR GIFT TO ME!

AH, MY CROP! I CAN—
YES! THERE!

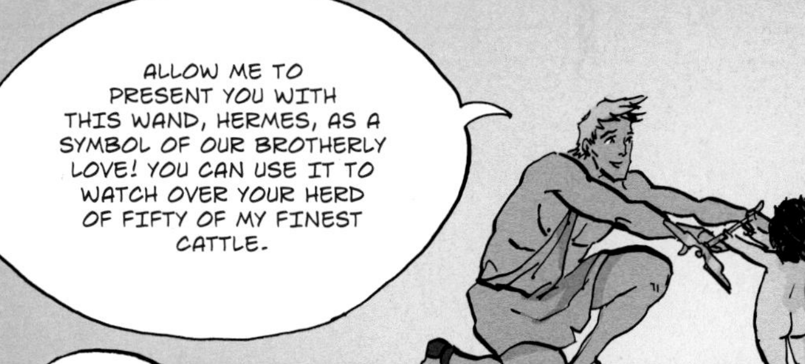
ALLOW ME TO PRESENT YOU WITH THIS WAND, HERMES, AS A SYMBOL OF OUR BROTHERLY LOVE! YOU CAN USE IT TO WATCH OVER YOUR HERD OF FIFTY OF MY FINEST CATTLE.

FORTY-EIGHT.
WHAT? THERE WERE—
IT'S PROBABLY BEST NOT TO ASK.

WELL, THAT SEEMS SETTLED.
APPROACH, MY SON.

I THINK I CAN SAY, WITHOUT FEAR OF DISAGREEMENT— WELCOME TO OLYMPUS, HERMES.

YOUR MOTHER— SHE'S MAIA, RIGHT?
YEP!
SHE ALWAYS WAS A SMART ONE.

IT'S CLEAR YOU'VE TALENTS IN ABUNDANCE, AND I'LL NEED TO ASSIGN YOU MANY DUTIES, TO KEEP YOU OCCUPIED AND STAVE OFF YOUR MORE... MISCHIEVOUS TENDENCIES.
SO, FIRST— A FEW MORE GIFTS TO AID YOU IN THE SWIFT COMPLETION OF YOUR DUTIES.

A WINGED HELMET TO REPLACE YOUR TORTOISE SHELL...

AND WINGED SANDALS TO PROTECT YOUR TENDER BABY FEET.

WHAT SAY YOU, HERMES?
JUST HAPPY TO BE ON THE TEAM, POP!

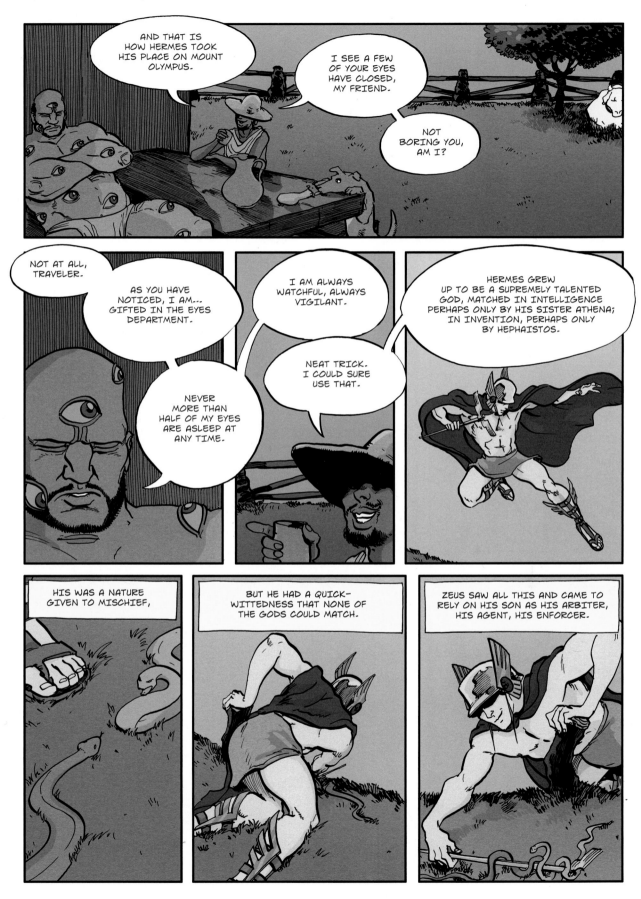

AND THAT IS HOW HERMES TOOK HIS PLACE ON MOUNT OLYMPUS.
I SEE A FEW OF YOUR EYES HAVE CLOSED, MY FRIEND.
NOT BORING YOU, AM I?

NOT AT ALL, TRAVELER.
AS YOU HAVE NOTICED, I AM... GIFTED IN THE EYES DEPARTMENT.
NEVER MORE THAN HALF OF MY EYES ARE ASLEEP AT ANY TIME.
I AM ALWAYS WATCHFUL, ALWAYS VIGILANT.
NEAT TRICK. I COULD SURE USE THAT.

HERMES GREW UP TO BE A SUPREMELY TALENTED GOD, MATCHED IN INTELLIGENCE PERHAPS ONLY BY HIS SISTER ATHENA; IN INVENTION, PERHAPS ONLY BY HEPHAISTOS.

HIS WAS A NATURE GIVEN TO MISCHIEF,

BUT HE HAD A QUICK-WITTEDNESS THAT NONE OF THE GODS COULD MATCH.

ZEUS SAW ALL THIS AND CAME TO RELY ON HIS SON AS HIS ARBITER, HIS AGENT, HIS ENFORCER.

AS LONG AS HE WAS KEPT BUSY, HERMES WAS THE GREATEST OF ASSETS.

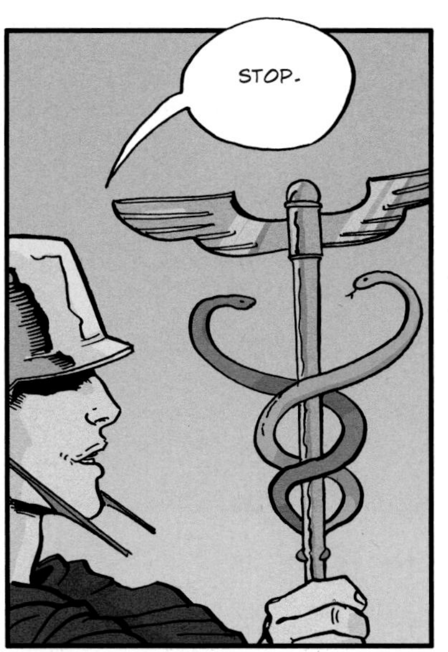
STOP.

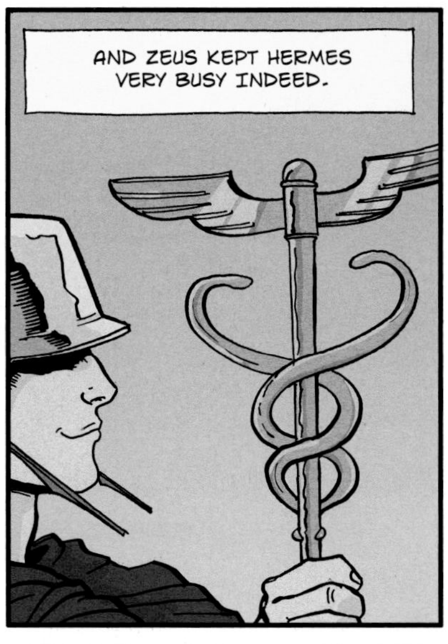
AND ZEUS KEPT HERMES VERY BUSY INDEED.

HE IS THE GOD OF PEACEMAKERS,

OF ASTRONOMY, OF CALENDARS,

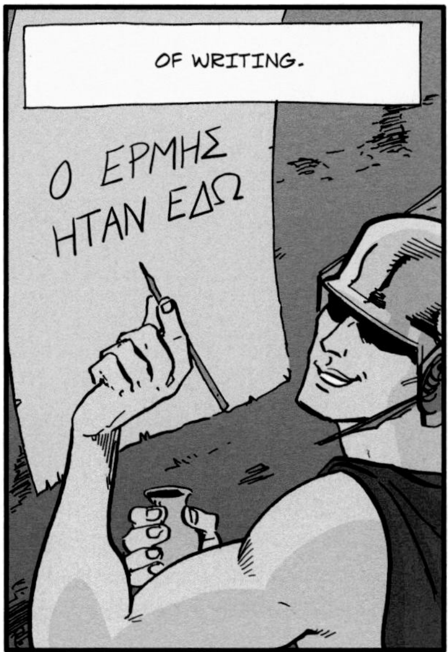
OF WRITING.
Ο ΕΡΜΗΣ ΗΤΑΝ ΕΔΩ

HE IS THE GOD OF THIEVES AND LIARS,

OF LANGUAGE AND ELOQUENCE,

OF POLITICIANS.

HE IS THE GOD OF MERCHANTS, OF TRADE,

OF HOSPITALITY,

OF TRAVEL, AND BOUNDARIES.

HERMES IS THE GOD WHO BRINGS YOU YOUR DREAMS EVERY NIGHT,

AND WHEN YOU DIE, HE IS THE GOD WHO WILL BRING YOU TO THE UNDERWORLD.

HE IS THE GOD OF ATHLETICS AND GYMNASIUMS,

OF THE HOME, AND OF GUARD DOGS.

HE'S THE GOD OF RUSTIC DIVINATION AND GAMBLING,

AND OF FLOCKS AND HERDS AND THOSE WHO WATCH OVER THEM.

WHY, A RUSTIC SETTING LIKE THIS WOULD BE THE PERFECT PLACE TO FIND HERMES!

HE COULD HELP YOU KEEP AN EYE ON YOUR HERD OVER THERE!
HEH-HEH.

IN ALL SERIOUSNESS, THOUGH, PERHAPS IT WAS HERMES'S ROLE AS GUARDIAN OF FLOCKS THAT LED TO HIS MOST-UNUSUAL CHILD.
AND, TO BE SURE, HERMES HAS HAD MANY UNUSUAL CHILDREN.

SUCH AS PRIAPUS, THE... VIGOROUS GOD OF FERTILITY.

AND HERMAPHRODITE, HERMES'S SON/DAUGHTER BY APHRODITE.

WINGED, MISCHIEVOUS EROS WAS PERHAPS ALSO HIS SON, THOUGH ONLY APHRODITE KNOWS FOR SURE, AND SHE ISN'T TELLING.

BUT IT WAS IN ANOTHER CAVE, ON ANOTHER MOUNTAIN IN ARCADIA...

AAAAAAH!

NURSE! WHAT IS IT? IS PENELOPE OKAY?!
AH—AH— THE BABY!

HE'S— HE'S INHUMAN!

AAAAHHH!

PENELOPE?
ARE YOU ALL RIGHT? THE NURS—
OVER HERE, HERMES. I'M FINE. AND THE BABY...

...HE TAKES AFTER YOU.

SAY HI TO OUR SON, HERMES.

HA!

HAHAHA!

HAHAHAHAHAHAHAHAHAHAHAHAHAHA

GUYSEVERYBODYCOMEQUICKYOUHAVETOSEE!

WEREN'T YOU JUST HERE?
LADY, I'VE ALWAYS JUST BEEN EVERYWHERE!

C'MON, EVERYONE—QUICK, GATHER AROUND.
HE WAS ONLY JUST BORN, HIS MOM IS GOING TO KILL ME, BUT I WANTED YOU ALL TO MEET—

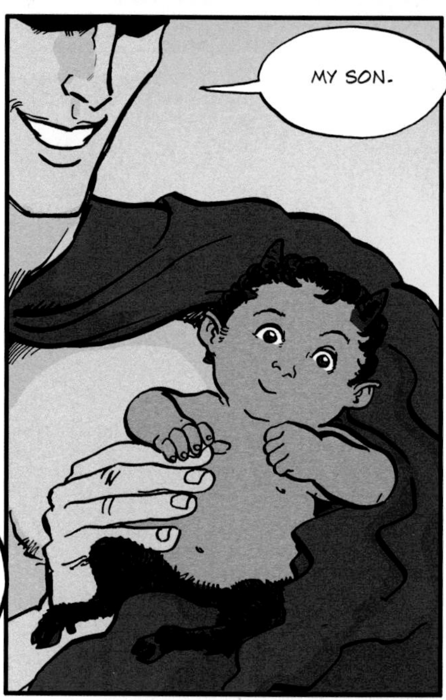
MY SON.

OOH, LOOK AT HIS LITTLE HORNS!
AND HIS LITTLE HOOVES!
ADORABLE.
EVERYONE, WATCH YOUR PURSES IF HE'S ANYTHING LIKE HIS FATHER.
HA!

POP! MEET YOUR GRANDSON! BORN IN A CAVE JUST LIKE YOU, JUST LIKE ME!
WELL!
NO ONE COULD EVER DENY THAT EVERYONE CERTAINLY LOVES YOU!

AND YOU CERTAINLY ARE HERMES'S SON.
BWAHAHA!

AND "PAN" BECAME HIS NAME, MEANING "ALL" OR "EVERYTHING"—AFTER ALL, AS ZEUS PROCLAIMED, EVERYONE ON OLYMPUS LOVED HIM.
ANOTHER FAMILY MIGHT HAVE SHUNNED HIM, BUT THE OLYMPIANS HAVE ALWAYS APPRECIATED THAT WHICH IS DIFFERENT.

BUT PAN, BY HIS VERY APPEARANCE, WAS OF TWO NATURES: HALF MAN, HALF GOAT. CIVILIZATION AND THE WILD. TWO WORLDS SIMULTANEOUSLY.

THIS DICHOTOMY DREW HIM TO THE FRINGES OF CIVILIZATION.
HIS CLOSEST COMPANION AMONG THE OLYMPIANS WAS THE SIMILARLY BORDERLINE DIONYSOS, AND PAN COULD OFTEN BE FOUND AMONG HIS RETINUE.

DRINKING AND CAVORTING AND...OTHER ACTIVITIES.
SYRINX! SLOW DOWN!

SYRINX, I LOVE YOU! I LOVE YOU!

"I LOVE YOU, I LOVE YOU."
WOULD THAT I WERE AN ECHO, THAT YOU MIGHT AT LAST HEAR FROM ME WHAT YOU WANT!

NO, THAT WOULD NEVER DO!
GIGGLE!

YOU WOULD HAVE TO MEAN IT!
WHOOP!
SPLASH!

SYRINX, MY LOVE? WHERE DID YOU GO?

SYRINX?
PAAAAN!
PAAAN, WHY DID YOU NOT LEAVE ME ALOOONE?

I PRAAAYED TO GRANDMOTHER EARTH THAT SHE TURN ME INTO REEDS, SO I COULD ESCAPE YOOOU...
HEE-HEE!

SHE'S GONE...
TURNED INTO REEDS RATHER THAN BE WITH ME...

TEE-HEE, HE THINKS HIMSELF ANOTHER APOLLO AND YOU A DAPHNE!
GO AND LEEEEEAVE ME, PAAAN...

I WILL, SYRINX...
BUT FIRST, I WILL FASHION MYSELF SOMETHING TO REMEMBER YOU BY...

A SET OF PIPES SO THAT I MAY ALWAYS BRING YOUR SWEET VOICE WITH ME...
HEH.

THAT MUSIC...
...SO BEAUTIFUL!
PERHAPS I—I WAS HASTY...

TO SCORN ONE WHO WOULD MAKE MUSIC SUCH AS THAT— FOR ME!

PAN! OH, PAN! I'M BACK! WAIT UP!
HEE-HEE!

LIKE HIS FATHER, PAN IS A PROTECTOR OF SHEPHERDS AND THEIR FLOCKS.

AND, ALSO LIKE HIS FATHER, PAN IS POSSESSED OF A CERTAIN MISCHIEVOUS BENT.

HIS CRY CAN INDUCE A PARTICULAR STATE—A PANIC—

THAT SETS HEARTS RACING AND FLOCKS TO SCATTER.

HOOOOO!
AND SETS DOGS TO HOWLING, I SUPPOSE.
I GUESS I HAVE BEEN DRONING ON AND ON...
WHAT ABOUT YOU, FRIEND? DO YOU HAVE PATIENCE FOR ANOTHER OF MY STORIES?
HMMM.
YES, I THINK I DO.

WELL, THE SUN HAS SET. PERHAPS IT'S TIME FOR A DARKER TALE THAN THE SORT I'VE SHARED SO FAR...

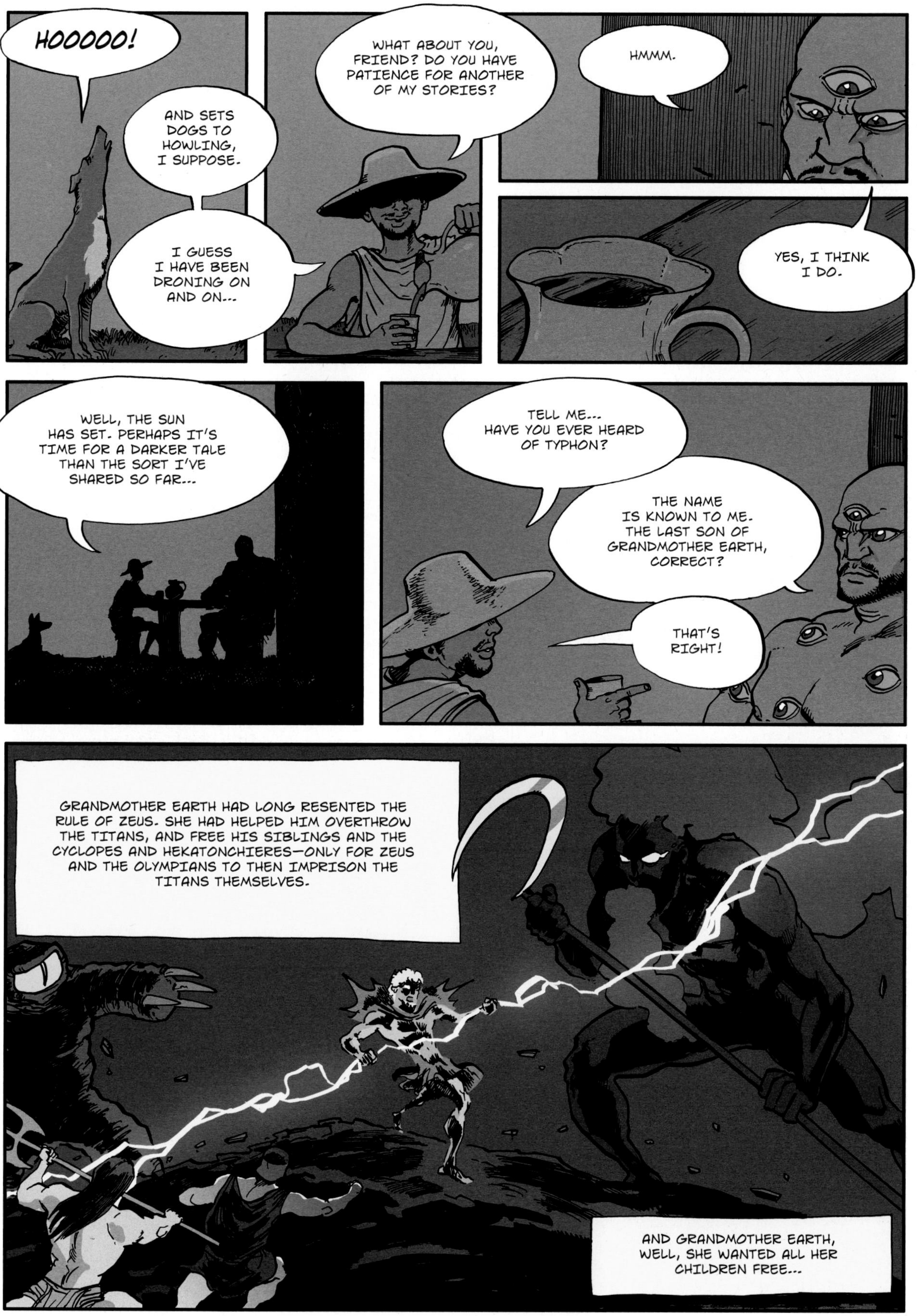

TELL ME... HAVE YOU EVER HEARD OF TYPHON?
THE NAME IS KNOWN TO ME. THE LAST SON OF GRANDMOTHER EARTH, CORRECT?
THAT'S RIGHT!

GRANDMOTHER EARTH HAD LONG RESENTED THE RULE OF ZEUS. SHE HAD HELPED HIM OVERTHROW THE TITANS, AND FREE HIS SIBLINGS AND THE CYCLOPES AND HEKATONCHIERES—ONLY FOR ZEUS AND THE OLYMPIANS TO THEN IMPRISON THE TITANS THEMSELVES.

AND GRANDMOTHER EARTH, WELL, SHE WANTED ALL HER CHILDREN FREE...

SHE HAD TRIED TO USURP THE OLYMPIAN ORDER BEFORE, UNSUCCESSFULLY.
SHE POURED ALL HER ENMITY, ALL HER MALICE, ALL HER WRATH AND SPITE INTO ONE LAST ATTEMPT.
ONE LAST CHILD.

A TERRIBLE MONSTER, A CREATURE OF STORMS, LIKE ZEUS, BUT UNFATHOMABLY, IMPOSSIBLY LARGER.

SO BIG, HE BLOTTED OUT THE SKY. HIS BLACK WINGS SCRAPED AGAINST THE STARS.

HIS HUNDRED HEADS BELCHED FORTH FIRE AND POISON AND OBSCENITIES IN ONE HUNDRED DIFFERENT TONGUES.

THIS CREATURE, TYPHON, TOOK THE SNAKE WOMAN ECHIDNA AS HIS WIFE.

AND I WONDER, FRIEND, IF *THAT* NAME RINGS A BELL AS WELL?
TOGETHER, TYPHON AND ECHIDNA POPULATED THE WORLD WITH MONSTERS. THESE CHILDREN FAVORED THEIR MOTHER AND FATHER TO VARYING DEGREES.

CERBERUS.
THE SPHINX.
THE NEMEAN LION.
LADON.
THE LERNAEAN HYDRA.
THE CHIMERA, AND MORE.

ZEUS AND THE REST OF THE OLYMPIANS KNEW OF THEM, OF COURSE.
THEY WEEDED OUT THE WORST ONES. TAMED SOME, SENT HEROES TO SLAY OTHERS. ALWAYS CAREFULLY, SO AS NOT TO AWAKE TYPHON.
UNTIL, ONE DAY, FINALLY, THE FURY OF TYPHON WAS LOOSED.

THE ENORMITY OF TYPHON LASHED THE OCEANS.

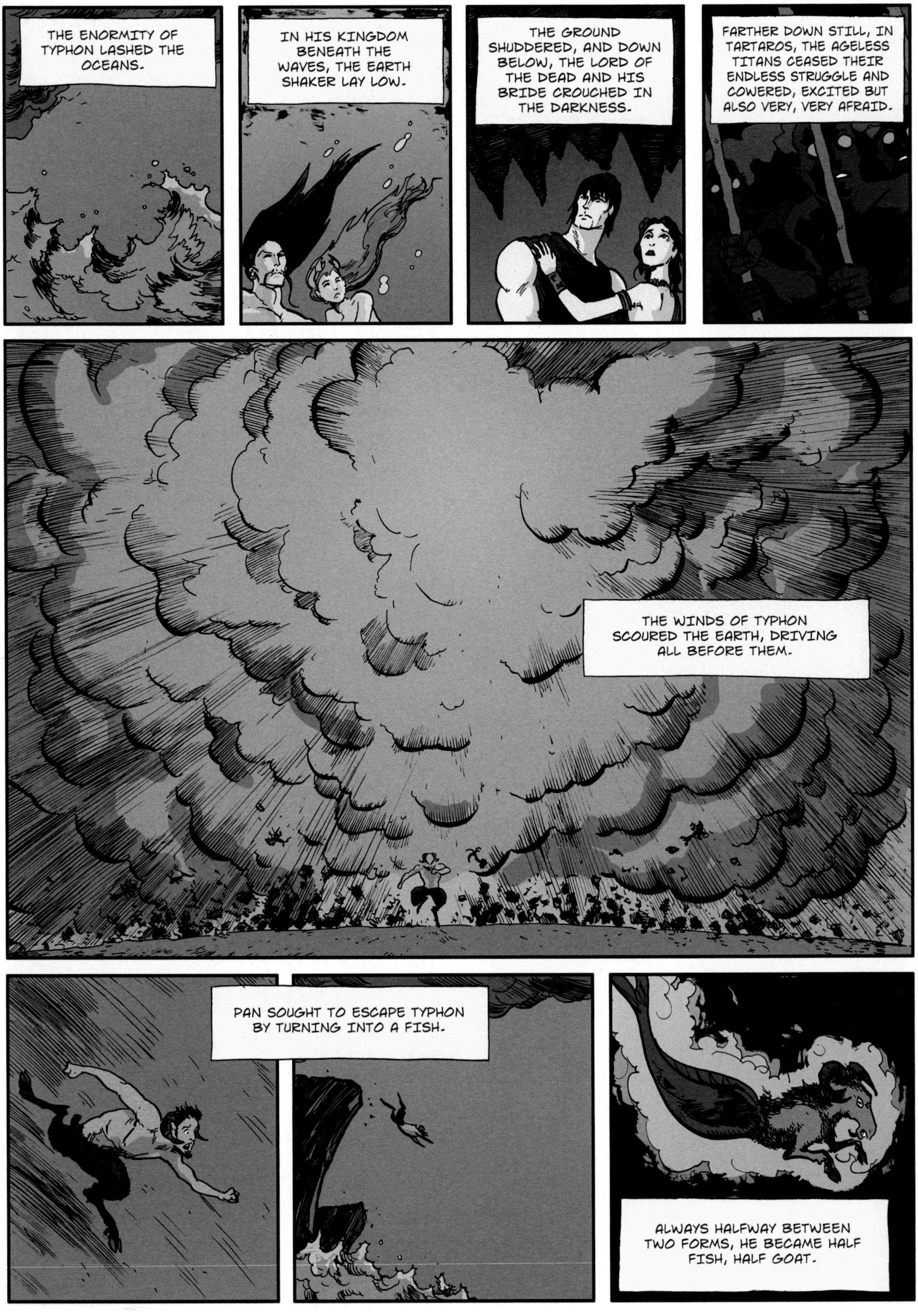

IN HIS KINGDOM BENEATH THE WAVES, THE EARTH SHAKER LAY LOW.

THE GROUND SHUDDERED, AND DOWN BELOW, THE LORD OF THE DEAD AND HIS BRIDE CROUCHED IN THE DARKNESS.

FARTHER DOWN STILL, IN TARTAROS, THE AGELESS TITANS CEASED THEIR ENDLESS STRUGGLE AND COWERED, EXCITED BUT ALSO VERY, VERY AFRAID.

THE WINDS OF TYPHON SCOURED THE EARTH, DRIVING ALL BEFORE THEM.

PAN SOUGHT TO ESCAPE TYPHON BY TURNING INTO A FISH.

ALWAYS HALFWAY BETWEEN TWO FORMS, HE BECAME HALF FISH, HALF GOAT.

AND ON OLYMPUS, THE TALLEST MOUNTAIN LEFT STANDING AFTER THE GODS' CLASH WITH THE TITANS...

THERE IS NOTHING TO BE GAINED BY STAYING HERE, FATHER. WE MUST LEAVE OLYMPUS—FOR NOW, NOT FOREVER...

BUT WE CAN MARSHAL OUR FORCES ELSEWHERE, PLAN A COUNTERSTRIKE. TAKE BACK OLYMPUS...

YEAH, POP, C'MON. PLEASE. WE CAN FIND SOMEPLACE FAR AWAY. LIE LOW UNTIL THE HEAT IS OFF.

NO. YOU GO; I'LL STAY AND FIGHT.
I SPENT ENOUGH OF MY LIFE HIDING IN DARKNESS.

ZEUS, PLEASE...
HE'S MADE UP HIS MIND, HERA. WE HAVE TO LEAVE.
BUT I'M COMING BACK FOR YOU, POP.

THE OLYMPIANS, SAVE ZEUS, TOOK ANIMAL FORMS AND FLED—

AS TYPHON ARRIVED. OVERWHELMING, IRRESISTIBLE, INDOMITABLE TYPHON.
YOUR FAMILY HAS DESERTED YOU, TINY ZEUS.
STOP COWERING IN YOUR LITTLE HOME. COME OUT AND FACE ME.
COME AND FACE YOUR RUIN.

I'M NOT AFRAID OF YOU, TYPHON!
K-KRAK!
I'M NOT THE WEAK STRIPLING GAIA ONCE HID AWAY—
I AM ZEUS! KING OF THE GODS!
AIIEE!

I DON'T CARE IF YOU HAVE ONE HUNDRED HEADS—
—OR ONE MILLION!
I'LL BURN THEM ALL, UNTIL ALL THAT REMAINS OF YOU IS BUT A SMOKING, BROKEN CINDER!
KRAK!

YOU MIGHT AT THAT, ZEUS—

HAD MOTHER SENT ME INTO BATTLE AGAINST YOU UNARMED...

...THE SICKLE OF KRONOS...

ARGHH!
PLLKT!

THOOM!

NOW, I CAN'T IMPRISON YOU, AND I CAN'T KILL YOU...
HOWEVER SHALL I CONTAIN YOU, ZEUS?

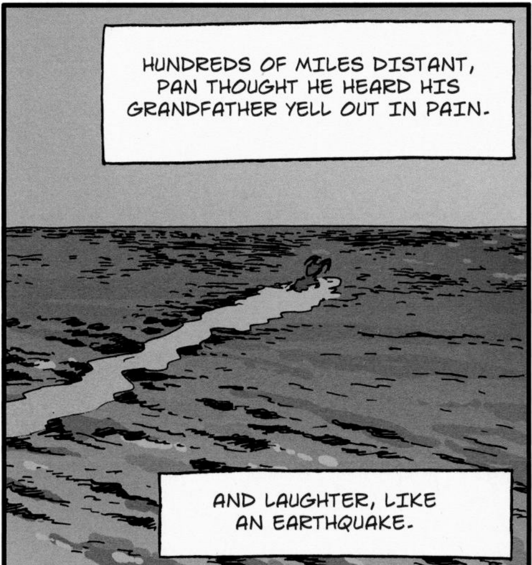
HUNDREDS OF MILES DISTANT, PAN THOUGHT HE HEARD HIS GRANDFATHER YELL OUT IN PAIN.
AND LAUGHTER, LIKE AN EARTHQUAKE.

AFRAID TO ABANDON HIS HALF FORM LEST TYPHON RECOGNIZE HIM, PAN MADE HIS WAY TO THE LAND THAT THE OLYMPIANS HAD FLED TO.

AT LAST.

THE GODS... SO DIFFERENT. THEY SEEM NOT TO NOTICE ME. BUT I KNOW THEM, EVEN IN THESE STRANGE FORMS.
APOLLO AND ARTEMIS.
QUEEN HERA AND HEPHAISTOS.

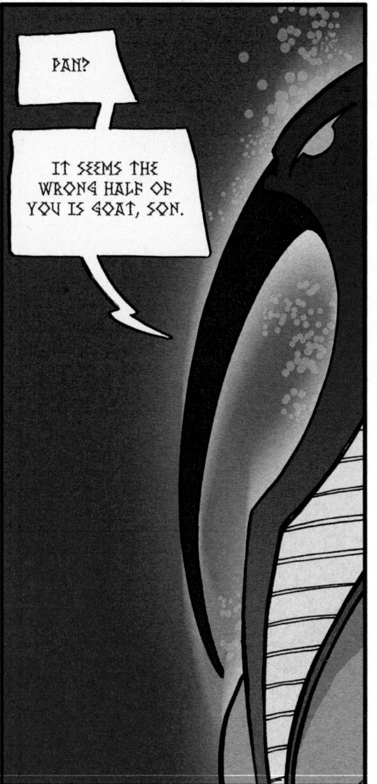

APHRODITE... AND MY FRIEND DIONYSOS!

AND...

YEAH, THAT WAS... STRANGE.

WE WORE ANIMAL FORMS WHEN WE CAME TO EGYPT, SINCE THAT'S HOW THEY KNOW US.

IT FELT VERY... REMOTE. AND DISTANT. BUT I'M BACK NOW.

IS GRANDFATHER HERE? I THOUGHT—

NO, HE STAYED BEHIND, TO FACE THAT HORROR ALONE.

I TOLD HIM I'D COME BACK FOR HIM...

AND COME BACK FOR ZEUS THEY DID.

DISGUISED AS TRAVELERS, HERMES AND PAN MADE THEIR WAY INTO GREECE.

THEY FOUND THE CRATER WHERE ZEUS HAD CRASHED BACK TO EARTH.

HE SURPRISED ME... WITH THE ADAMANTINE SICKLE OF KRONOS, MY FATHER...
CUT OUT MY SINEWS...

...WRAPPED THEM IN BEAR SKIN, AND TOOK THEM TO HIS CAVE...

...LEFT ME THIS EMPTY PUPPET...

GET THEM BACK FOR ME. HE WON'T SURPRISE ME AGAIN...
NEXT TIME, I'LL BEAT HIM.
SURE THING, POP. I HAVE A PLAN...

IN ANOTHER CAVE, ON ANOTHER MOUNTAIN, THIS TIME IN FAR-OFF SCYTHIA...

THIS WAS WHERE TYPHON SLUMBERED ATOP THE SINEWS OF THE KING OF THE GODS.
IT WAS NOT A PLACE THAT USUALLY HAD VISITORS.

SOME SAY THE VISITOR WAS SELLING FISH, BUT WHAT USE HAS ONE SUCH AS TYPHON FOR A FISHERMAN'S CATCH?
I PREFER TO THINK THE VISITOR PLAYED A TUNE. MAYBE ON SOME REED PIPES?

WHATEVER THE VISITOR DID, HOWEVER, IT WORKED.

HE DREW OUT THE GREAT BEAST, LIKE POISON DRAWN FROM A WOUND.

MORE AND MORE, UNTIL THE NOONTIME SUN WAS BLACKENED COMPLETELY.

TYPHON, LOOMING SUSPENDED IN THE SKY. FILLING THE SKY.

AND THEN?

WHATEVER IT WAS, IT WORKED—FOR THE MEREST OF MOMENTS, TYPHON WAS STARTLED. EVEN SCARED.

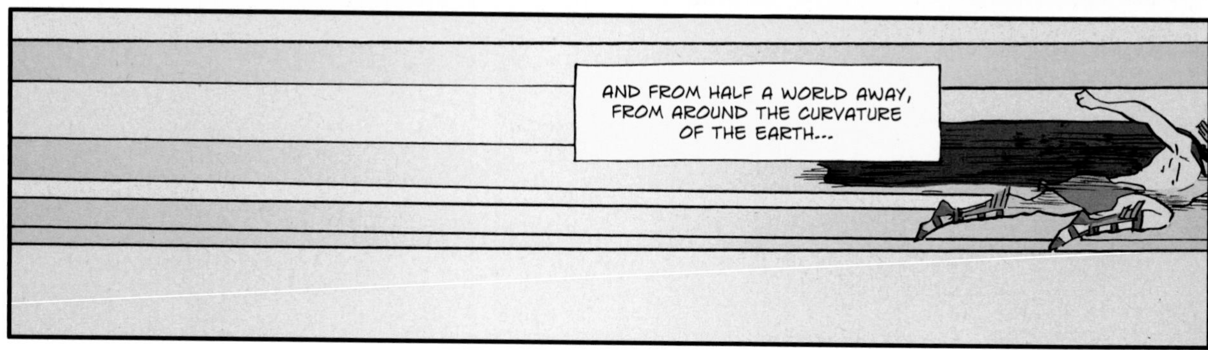

BEFORE TYPHON COULD EVEN REACT.

HERMES STOLE IN, SNATCHED HIS FATHER'S SINEWS...

AND THEN ZEUS, KING OF THE GODS WAS WHOLE AGAIN.

AND HE WAS ***ANGRY***.

ZEUS BURNED FIFTY OF TYPHON'S HEADS, OR MORE.
SPEARED HIS LIGHTNING BOLT THROUGH TYPHON'S MIDDLE, PINNING HIM TO GRANDMOTHER EARTH.
RIPPED LOOSE A MOUNTAIN FROM THE EARTH'S MANTLE.

AND BURIED TYPHON BENEATH IT.

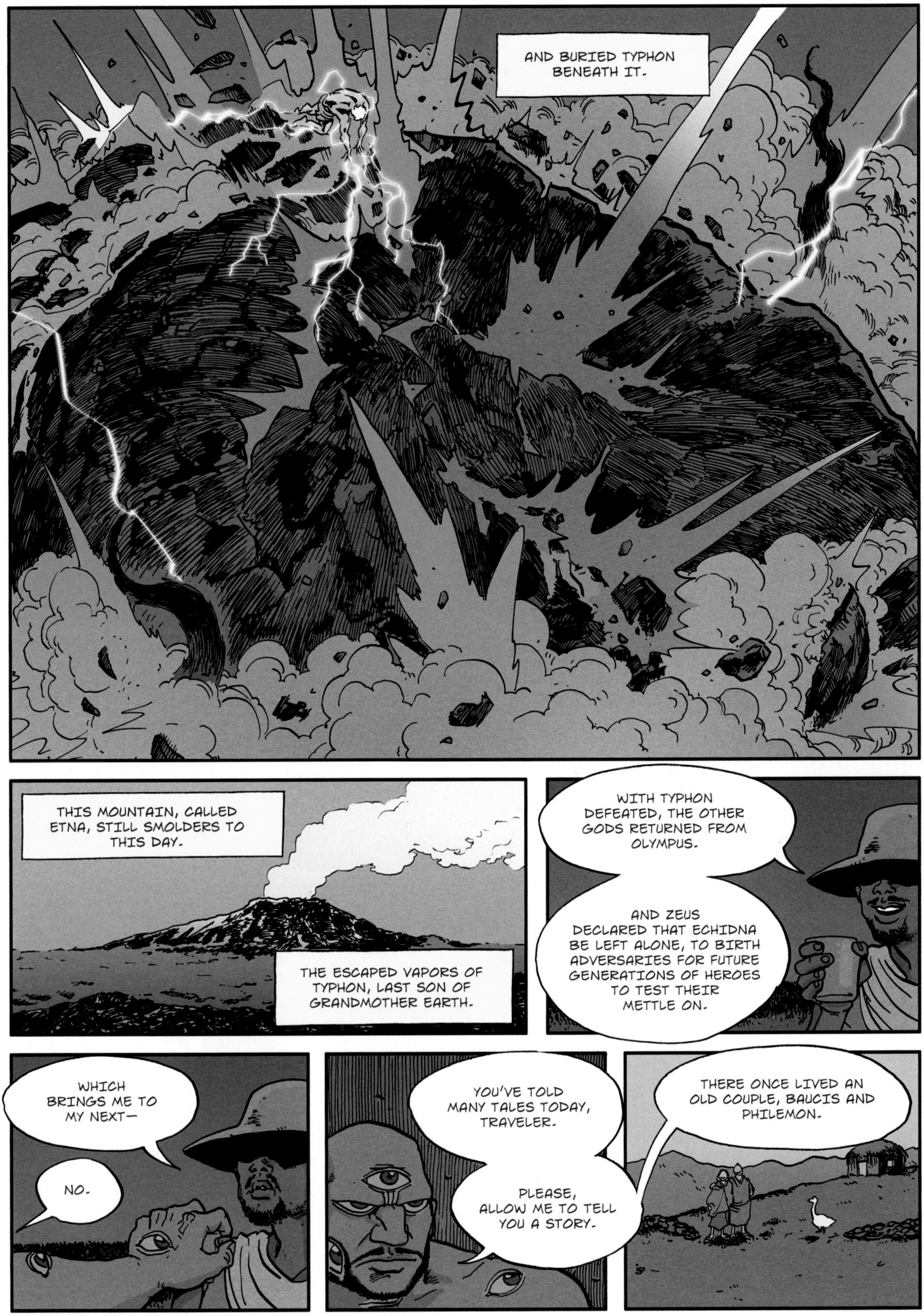

THIS MOUNTAIN, CALLED ETNA, STILL SMOLDERS TO THIS DAY.
THE ESCAPED VAPORS OF TYPHON, LAST SON OF GRANDMOTHER EARTH.

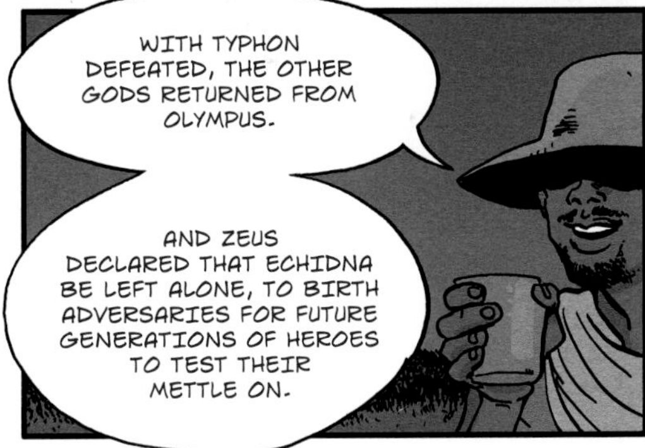

WITH TYPHON DEFEATED, THE OTHER GODS RETURNED FROM OLYMPUS.
AND ZEUS DECLARED THAT ECHIDNA BE LEFT ALONE, TO BIRTH ADVERSARIES FOR FUTURE GENERATIONS OF HEROES TO TEST THEIR METTLE ON.

WHICH BRINGS ME TO MY NEXT—
NO.

YOU'VE TOLD MANY TALES TODAY, TRAVELER.
PLEASE, ALLOW ME TO TELL YOU A STORY.

THERE ONCE LIVED AN OLD COUPLE, BAUCIS AND PHILEMON.

ONE DAY, TWO TRAVELERS CAME TO THEIR HUMBLE COTTAGE, SEEKING HOSPITALITY.
THEY HAD BEEN TO ALL OF BAUCIS AND PHILEMON'S NEIGHBORS BUT WERE TURNED AWAY.

THE ELDERLY COUPLE INVITED THE TRAVELERS IN, AND SHARED WHAT MEAGER FOOD AND WINE THEY HAD.

THEY MADE SURE NO ONE'S CUP WAS EVER EMPTY, THOUGH MANY WERE PRACTICALLY DRAINED. THEN BAUCIS NOTICED THEIR PITCHER WAS STILL FILLED TO THE BRIM WITH WINE.

LIKE YOUR CUP TONIGHT. LIKE THIS PITCHER.

WELL, I'LL BE.

IT WAS THEN THAT BAUCIS AND PHILEMON KNEW THEY HAD BEEN ENTERTAINING GODS. THEY BEGGED FORGIVENESS FOR THEIR MODEST PROVISIONS.
PHILEMON WANTED TO SLAUGHTER THEIR ONLY GOOSE, TO MAKE A MORE WORTHY MEAL.

BUT ZEUS AND HERMES, FOR IT WAS THEY WHO HAD BEEN DISGUISED AS TRAVELERS, SAID THERE WAS NO NEED. INSTEAD, THE COUPLE SHOULD COME WITH THEM.

AND BRING THAT GOOSE ALONG, TOO.

BAUCIS AND PHILEMON FOLLOWED THE TWO GODS UP A NEARBY MOUNTAIN.

THEY REACHED THE TOP, AND ZEUS BADE THEM TURN AROUND.

THEIR WHOLE VILLAGE, ALL THEIR NEIGHBORS, WAS GONE—SWEPT AWAY IN A FLOOD. THE COUPLE HAD BEEN SPARED BECAUSE OF THE KINDNESS THEY HAD SHOWN THE GODS.
MOREOVER, ZEUS WOULD GRANT THEM WHATEVER THEY WISHED. BUT BAUCIS AND PHILEMON WANTED NO RICHES, NO PALACES.

THEY JUST WISHED THAT WHEN IT WAS TIME FOR ONE OF THEM TO DIE, THEY BOTH WOULD, TOGETHER.
FOR MY PART, I HAVE NO WISH TO DIE. BUT I SEE WHO YOU ARE, AND I CANNOT STAND AGAINST AN OLYMPIAN.
I SEE YOU KNOW THAT COW IS REALLY IO, A LOVE OF ZEUS'S, TURNED INTO A HEIFER. THE LADY HERA SET ME TO WATCH OVER HER.

I SEE YOU KNOW I AM ARGUS PANOPTES, THE ALL-SEEING, THE SLAYER OF ECHIDNA, THE WIDOW OF TYPHON.

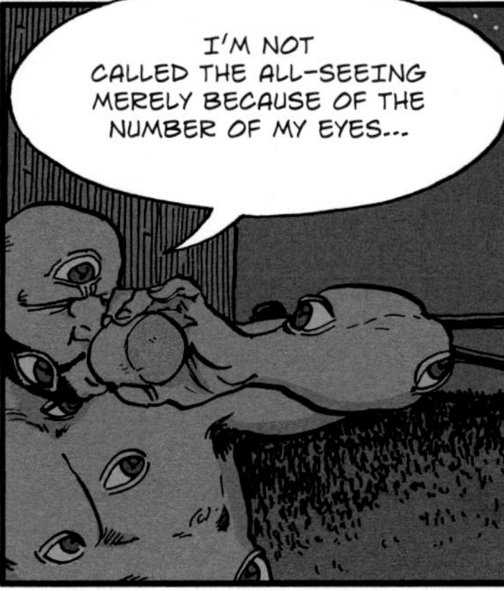
I'M NOT CALLED THE ALL-SEEING MERELY BECAUSE OF THE NUMBER OF MY EYES...

...LORD HERMES.

I HAVE NO IDEA WHAT YOU'RE TALKING ABOUT.

COME OFF IT! ALL THESE STORIES OF HERMES, OF COWS, OF GODS IN DISGUISE! YOU'RE HERMES, COME TO TAKE IO!

ACTUALLY, HE'S TELLING THE TRUTH.
TRUST ME. I'M A BIT OF AN AUTHORITY ON LIES.

DOG! YOU'RE TALKING TO HIM NOW, TOO?
SHHH, AESOP. SLEEP.

ZZZZZZZZ

HE WASN'T KIDDING BEFORE, WHEN HE SAID I TOLD HIM THAT DOG AMBASSADORS STORY.
I'M THE GOD OF FABLES, TOO. THAT'S ONE HE LEFT OFF THE LIST.
HOLD ON A SECOND, WHILE I SLIP INTO SOMETHING MORE COMFORTABLE.

AH, BETTER!
ANYWAY, MY TRAVELING COMPANION WAS SUPPOSED TO PUT YOU TO SLEEP WITH HIS STORIES, BUT THEY WERE JUST TOO DARN EXCITING!

IT MAKES SENSE, I GUESS. I TOLD HIM MOST OF THEM MYSELF.
SORRY ABOUT THIS, ARGUS. YOU SEEM LIKE A REALLY NICE GUY, AND I'M USUALLY NICER TO THOSE WHO SHOW KINDNESS TO STRANGERS.

YOU SHOULDN'T HAVE TO SEE THIS COMING.
SLEEEEEP...

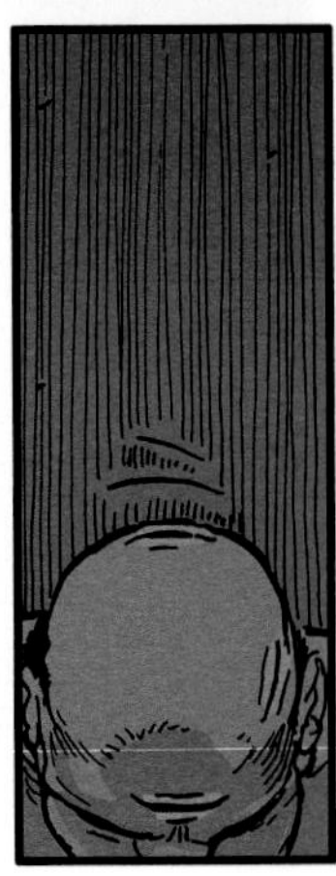

POOR ARGUS...
BUT YOU REALLY SHOULDN'T HAVE KILLED ECHIDNA. ZEUS SAID SHE WAS OFF-LIMITS.
NOW, AS FOR YOU, IO...

IF THERE IS ONE THING I KNOW—
AND I KNOW MANY, MANY, *MANY* THINGS—
IT'S THAT YOUR STORY IS NOT YET OVER, IO.

JUST THIS CHAPTER.
YOU'RE FREE. STILL A COW, HOWEVER. SORRY.

I'D HOOF IT IF I WERE YOU. HERA'S GOING TO BE PLENTY MAD WHEN SHE SEES WHAT I DID TO ARGUS.
MAYBE TRY EGYPT? IT'S A NICE PLACE, TRUST ME.

YOU STILL HAVE A WHILE TO GO, POOR IO.
BUT THAT'S A STORY FOR ANOTHER DAY.

EPILOGUE

SIGHHH. WHEREVER ARE YOU, IO?

IT'S NOT HARD TO GUESS WHO FREED YOU. I GUESS HE'S TOO BUSY THESE DAYS TO TIE BARK TO YOUR HOOVES.

HERE'S A GADFLY, IO, TO SPEED YOU ON YOUR WAY.
TRY RELAXING WITH THAT STINGING AT YOUR HAUNCHES.

AND ARGUS, MY FAITHFUL SERVANT— YOU DESERVED BETTER THAN THIS.

I WANT TO HONOR YOUR SACRIFICE, YOUR UNDYING VIGILANCE...
AH! I KNOW HOW.

NOW YOUR HUNDRED EYES WILL STARE ON FOREVERMORE.

ZEUS WAS SMART TO SEND HERMES TO DO THIS.

I JUST CAN'T STAY MAD AT THAT GUY.

Listen closely, because this is my origin story.

I was Hermes when I was in third grade.

I mean, not literally. That would be crazy. For starters, I'm pretty sure there was no such thing as third grade when Hermes was born. No, in third grade, I was actually a student at Tackan Elementary in Nesconset, part of Long Island in New York. I was a good student, though maybe one who spent a little too much time drawing musclemen, monsters, and pretty ladies rather than paying attention in class. At another time, in another place, I might even have become one of those students who slips through the cracks of the education system. A quiet little dreamer who lost himself in his imagined worlds.

However, in third grade I was put into a pilot education program called STEPS. If I ever knew what STEPS stood for, I do not any longer. But whatever it meant, STEPS was a building block of my young personality. In STEPS, we studied subjects in an immersive manner—we would spend weeks, sometimes even months, approaching subjects from multiple angles. Creative and unorthodox solutions were encouraged, and assignments were project- rather than testing-based. Every day we would sit in a circle and spend time just writing whatever popped into our heads—in journals we had sewed together ourselves. We learned how to research, and how to speak in public without looking like we were reading off cards. We studied Rube Goldberg machines, portmanteaus, the Iroquois and Algonquin peoples.

We studied Greek mythology.

This was a different time, before Rick Riordan, but as the class's resident muscleman-and-monster drawer, I still knew a little bit about Greek mythology. I knew who Zeus was, for instance, and Hercules (Heracles!) and the minotaur, and that guy with the wings on his head—what was his name again?

Oh yeah, Hermes.

Hermes quickly became my favorite. He was smart, funny, and clever, and a little bit of a troublemaker but in a (mostly) mischievous, not malicious, way. In school, I'd not fit in, I had been quiet and withdrawn, but in my heart, at home, I was like Hermes. In studying the Greek gods, I found a topic that inspired me, and through that inspiration I discovered how to express the true me. At the conclusion of our Greek mythology unit, each of the students in STEPS had to dress up as their favorite Greek god and deliver an oral report to the rest of the class. I stood there before a room of my peers, with a winged baseball cap, a green-paper-snake-and-coat-hanger caduceus, wearing a towel around my waist and with looseleaf wings taped to my feet.

"Hermes was the greatest Greek god because..."

And the rest is history.

George O'Connor
Brooklyn, NY
2017

HERMES

TRICKSTER GOD

SACRED PLANTS The Crocus, the Strawberry Tree

SACRED PLACES Arcadia (place of his birth and his childhood). Roads (stone markers called "herms" were set up for the god throughout ancient Greece). As one of the most familiar and friendiest of the Olympians, most homes had a small shrine to Hermes.

DAY OF THE WEEK Wednesday

MONTH May (named after his mother, Maia)

HEAVENLY BODY The planet Mercury

MODERN LEGACIES Images of Hermes are still very common today, with many companies (Goodyear, FTD) having logos depicting the god.

The element mercury, used in thermometers, derives its name from his Roman version.

Befitting the god of trickery, his caduceus is widely used as a symbol of medicine or healing; this is due to it being mistaken as the similar-looking rod of Asklepios, the Greek god of healing.

GOD OF (Are you ready?) Boundaries, Shepherds, Travel, Roads, Hospitality, Diplomacy, Trade, Merchants, Invention, Thieves, Orators, Wit, Cunning, Language, Writing, Measurements, Astrology, Astronomy, Sleep, Dreams, Magic, Fertility, Athletics, Gymnasiums, and much, much more

ROMAN NAME Mercury

SYMBOLS Winged Sandals, Winged Helmet, the Caduceus (his winged staff)

SACRED ANIMALS Ram, Tortoise (Hermes made the first lyre from the shell of one)

GREEK NOTES

PAGE 1, PANEL 1: The song that the Mysterious Traveler is singing here is the "Seikilos Epitaph," the oldest surviving complete musical composition in the world. These lyrics, with accompanying musical notation, were found inscribed on a tombstone in Turkey.

PAGE 1, PANELS 2–4: The statue of Hermes that the Traveler is addressing is a herm—a (usually) square stone pillar with a bust of Hermes carved atop it. They were used at crossroads or as boundary markers of territories throughout the Greek and Latin speaking world. The dog, ahem, "saluting" the herm is a reference to a fable by Aesop (#308 in the Perry Index), *Hermes and the Dog.*

PAGE 2, PANEL 3: Longtime readers of OLYMPIANS will recognize the jewelry-wearing cow as none other than Io, introduced in Book 3, *Hera: The Goddess and Her Glory.*

PAGE 4, PANEL 5: Anachronistic chronometer jokes: just one of many reasons you return to OLYMPIANS for your entertainment dollar.

PAGE 7, PANEL 4: I prefer cats.

PAGE 9, PANEL 2: We last saw Atlas, hard at work in keeping the sky from falling, in OLYMPIANS Book 3, *Hera: The Goddess and Her Glory.*

PAGE 9, PANELS 6–7: Zeus's being raised in a cave occurs in OLYMPIANS Book 1, *Zeus: King of the Gods.* Zeus's swallowing of Metis occurs in OLYMPIANS Book 2, *Athena: Grey-Eyed Goddess.* The hounding of Leto occurs in OLYMPIANS Books 8 and 9, *Apollo: The Brilliant One* and *Artemis: Wild Goddess of the Hunt.*

PAGE 10, PANEL 1: Ten books into the series, and we finally get to see Hermes's eyes. This was deliberate on my part—the best way to tell when someone is lying is to stare into their eyes. As the god of liars, Hermes ain't ever going to let you do that.

PAGE 12, PANEL 4: If you're a newborn infant planning on running all over the earth at supersonic speeds in the dead of night, be like Hermes and wear a helmet, for goodness' sake.

PAGE 14, PANEL 2: This is the astrological symbol of the sun and, by extension, Apollo.

PAGE 16, PANEL 4: I love how over the top baby Hermes is in coming up with all the different ways to disguise the tracks of Apollo's cows. Also, the giant feet he straps on here are the most plausible explanation I've seen yet for Sasquatch.

PAGE 18: This story with the dates and almonds is another reference to an Aesop's fable (#178 in the Perry Index), *The Traveller and Hermes.*

PAGE 20, PANEL 2: As goddess of the hunt, Artemis knows her stuff.

PAGE 21, PANELS 9–10: God logic.

PAGES 23–27: Stop right now. Go to YouTube, look up something called "yakety sax," press play, and read these four pages with that as your soundtrack. In an ideal world, each volume of OLYMPIANS would be an unlimited number of pages, and this chase sequence would extend for, like, eighty-eight pages.

PAGE 24, PANEL 3: The Dogheads are the cynocephali, a mythical race of dog-headed humans.

PAGE 24, PANEL 4: The Bigfoot here is a skiapod, one of a mythical race of men who use their one giant foot as an umbrella from the sweltering sun.

PAGE 33, PANELS 6–7: Hermes's pose in these two panels is taken from the statue *Mercure Invente le Caducee (Mercury Inventing the Caduceus)* by the French sculptor Antonin Idrac. It's one of my all-time favorite sculptures—in fact, when you enter my house, a photo of this sculpture is the first thing you see.

PAGE 34, PANEL 3: I mention this in the Greek notes for OLYMPIANS Book 8, *Apollo: The Brilliant One*, but it's worth addressing here as well. In many places in the world, particularly if you live in the United States of America, you might be familiar with the wand of Hermes (called the "kerykeion" or "caduceus") as a symbol of medicine. That's because Hermes the trickster stole this job from the rod of Asklepios, god of healing.

PAGE 35, PANEL 3: Hermes's pose in this panel is taken from yet another favorite statue of mine, *Un secret d'en Haut* (A Secret from on High) by Hippolyte Moulin.

PAGE 36, PANEL 6: We previously met Eros, and learned of his uncertain parentage, in OLYMPIANS Book 6, *Aphrodite: Goddess of Love.*

PAGE 37, PANEL 5: This Penelope should not be confused with Penelope the famously faithful wife of Odysseus, from *The Odyssey*, though much better writers than I (like Herodotus and Apollodorus, among others) did just that.

PAGE 37, PANEL 9: Déjà vu.

PAGE 40, PANEL 3: "Would that I were an echo"—this is in reference to the nymph Echo, another love of Pan's, a nymph who was cursed by Hera to only be able to repeat what was said to her by others.

PAGE 41, PANEL 4: You can read the story of Apollo and Daphne in OLYMPIANS Book 8, *Apollo: The Brilliant One.*

PAGE 42, PANEL 5: The word "panic" literally comes from Pan's yell! Isn't that neat? I think it's neat!!

PAGE 43, PANELS 3–4: Hmmm, indeed.

PAGE 43, PANEL 7: You can see the battle of the gods and the Titans, aka the Titanomachy, in OLYMPIANS Book 1, *Zeus: King of the Gods.*

PAGE 45, PANEL 1: Just gonna toot my own horn here—I'm really pleased with my design of Echidna.

PAGE 45, PANEL 4: Lessee... We've met the Hydra, the Nemean Lion, Ladon, and Cerberus before, in OLYMPIANS Book 3, *Hera: The Goddess and Her Glory* (and Cerberus also appears in Book 4, *Hades: Lord of the Dead*). This is the first appearance in the series of the Sphinx and the Chimera, though. Hope I get to draw both of them some more!

PAGE 46, PANEL 2: Somehow I never squeezed her into OLYMPIANS Book 5, *Poseidon: Earth Shaker*, but that's his queen, Amphitrite, next to the moody king of the seas.

PAGE 46, PANEL 8: If your zodiac sign is Capricorn, now you know where that weird fish goat came from.

PAGES 48–49: Typhon is about as metal as they come.

PAGES 50–51: Actually, Zeus is pretty metal, too.

PAGE 52, PANEL 4: Now you know where the sickle of Kronos went, last seen in OLYMPIANS Book 1, *Zeus: King of the Gods*.

PAGE 53, PANEL 4: Back when they were first constructed, the great pyramids of Giza were clad in limestone, giving them a gleaming appearance.

PAGES 54–55, PANEL 1: You might be asking yourself right now, "Wait, I thought I was reading a book about *Greek* mythology?" Bam! Surprise Greek-Egyptian crossover! Well, not really, this is just the Greek myth to explain the Egyptian gods—that they were just the Olympians in disguise. For your edification, Apollo is Horus, Artemis is Bastet, Hera is Hathor, Hephaistos is Ptah, Aphrodite is Astarte, Dionysos is Heryshaf, and Hermes is Thoth.

PAGE 60: Okay, Zeus is officially the most metal.

PAGE 63, PANEL 6: Again, tooting my own horn here. I gotta find someplace else to draw my design of Echidna.

PAGE 64: Psych! You all thought the traveler is Hermes in disguise, didn't you? Tricked you! The traveler was none other than Aesop, he of Aesop's fables fame. Philostratus tells a story of how Aesop was bestowed with the gift of fable by Hermes himself. Accordingly, Hermes appears in Aesop's fables more than any other Olympian.

PAGE 65, PANEL 1: This panel reflects the composition of Diego Velázquez's awesome painting, *Mercury and Argus*.

PAGE 65, PANELS 5–6: "You still have a while to go, poor Io. But that's a story for another day." She sure does. Story to be continued in a future volume of OLYMPIANS!

ARGUS PANOPTES

THE WATCHFUL GUARDIAN

SACRED ANIMAL The hundred eyes of Argus Panoptes live on in the tail of the peacock, the sacred bird of Hera.

SACRED PLACE The Argolis, a region of the Peloponnese, was home to Argus (and is presumably the source of his name).

HEAVENLY BODIES The Search for Extra Terrestrial Life (SETI) has a program named Argus after this giant. It is a coordinated network of over five thousand individual radio telescopes (like Argus Panoptes's many eyes) monitor the heavens for signs of intelligent life.

MODERN LEGACY The Argus retinal prosthesis is a type of "bionic eye" that is implanted in the eye to improve the vision of people with certain degenerative vision disorders.

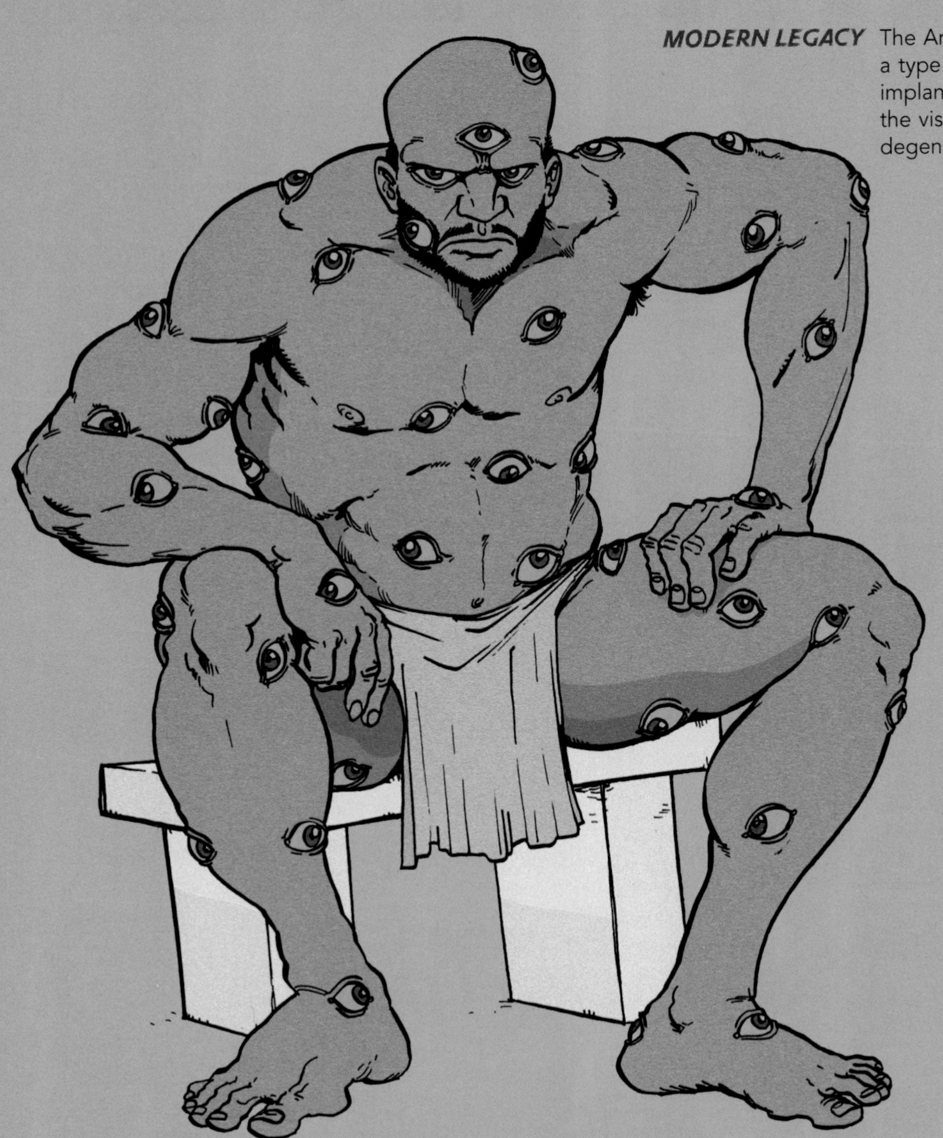

PAN

BELOVED BY ALL

GOD OF Shepherds, Flocks, the Wild

ROMAN NAME Faunus

SYMBOL The Syrinx, or Pan pipes

SACRED ANIMAL Goat (for obvious reasons)

SACRED PLANT The Syrinx Reed (water reeds)

SACRED PLACE Arcadia (his birthplace)

HEAVENLY BODY 4450 Pan, an asteroid

MODERN LEGACIES Modern words such as "panic" and "pandemonium" have their roots in this wild and unruly god.

Pan has appeared quite a bit in classic children's literature. He is the Piper at the Gates of Dawn in Kenneth Grahame's The *Wind in the Willows*, J.M. Barrie's Peter Pan takes his name from this god.

ABOUT THIS BOOK

HERMES: TALES OF THE TRICKSTER is the tenth book in *Olympians*, a graphic novel series from First Second that retells the Greek myths.

FOR DISCUSSION

1. It's strange that one of the first acts of Hermes, one of the most benevolent gods, is to take a life, even if it is just that of a turtle. Why do you think he does this?

2. What do you think is the significance of Zeus, Hermes, and Pan all being raised in caves?

3. Hermes sure is the god of many things. What are some other, more modern things that he might be the god of today?

4. Why do you think everyone on Olympus loves Pan so much?

5. You've already seen how the ancient Greeks matched up some of the Olympians with some of the Egyptian gods. What other Olympians might match up with what other Egyptian gods? What Olympians might match up with gods of other pantheons?

6. Why do you think Hermes kills Argus Panoptes?

7. Why do you suppose Pan was born half goat?

8. Hermes is the god of fables. What is it about Hermes that would make him the god of fables?

9. Very few people still worship the Olympian gods today. Why do you think it is important we still learn about them?

BIBLIOGRAPHY

EDITED AND TRANSLATED BY ML WEST. HOMERIC HYMNS. HOMERIC APOCRYPHA. LIVES OF HOMER
LOEB CLASSICAL LIBRARY, CAMBRIDGE, MA. HARVARD UNIVERSITY PRESS, 2007.
This was my primary source for the tale of tricksy baby Hermes and his punking of big bro Apollo.

METAMORPHOSES. ***OVID. TRANSLATED BY DAVID RAEBURN. NEW YORK: PENGUIN CLASSICS, 2004.***
This was my main source for the tales of Baucis and Philemon, Argus Panoptes, Syrinx and Pan, and the flight of the gods to Egypt, among others. *Metamorphoses* is a Roman text, so Hermes is called Mercury throughout, yet oddly, in this translation at least, Pan is still Pan.

AESOP'S FABLES. ***TRANSLATED BY LAURA GIBBS. NEW YORK: OXFORD UNIVERSITY PRESS, 2002.***
I went to the well of Aesop quite a few times in this book, and Gibb's translations of early Aesop's fables were extremely helpful.

APOLLODORUS, THE LIBRARY, VOLUME 1. ***PSEUDO-APOLLODORUS, NEW YORK: LOEB CLASSICAL LIBRARY, 1921.***
I got one of the accounts of Zeus's battle with Typhon from pseudo-Apollodorus, *whoever you really are...*

HESIOD: VOLUME 1, THEOGENY. WORKS AND DAYS: TESTIMONIA. ***HESIOD, NEW YORK: LOEB CLASSICAL LIBRARY, 2007.***
I'm pretty sure I list this as a source in almost every volume of OLYMPIANS, and for good reason: Hesiod is one of the core foundations of Greek mythology.

THEOI GREEK MYTHOLOGY WEB SITE. ***WWW.THEOI.COM***
Without a doubt, the single most valuable resource I came across in this entire venture. At Theoi.com, you can find an encyclopedia of various gods and goddesses from Greek mythology, cross-referenced with every mention of them they could find in literally hundreds of ancient Greek and Roman texts. Unfortunately, it's not quite complete, and it doesn't seem to be updated anymore.

MYTH INDEX WEB SITE. ***WWW.MYTHINDEX.COM***
Another mythology Web site connected to Theoi.com. While it doesn't have the painstakingly compiled quotations from ancient texts, it does offer some impressive encyclopedic entries on virtually every character to ever pass through a Greek myth. Pretty amazing.

ALSO RECOMMENDED

FOR YOUNGER READERS

D'Aulaires' Book of Greek Myths. Ingri and Edgar Parin D'Aulaire. New York: Doubleday, 1962.

I Am Pan! Mordicai Gerstein. New York: Roaring Brook Press, 2016.

FOR OLDER READERS

The Marriage of Cadmus and Harmony. Robert Calasso. New York: Knopf, 1993.

Mythology. Edith Hamilton. New York: Grand Central Publishing, 1999.

Trickster Makes This World. Lewis Hyde. New York: Farrar, Straus and Giroux, 1998.

The Infinities. John Banville. London: Picador, 2009.

AND ESPECIALLY RECOMMENDED FOR OLYMPIANS COMPLETISTS

Fable Comics. Edited by Chris Duffy. New York: First Second, 2015.
There are four, count 'em, four mini-Olympians comics in here by yours truly and starring that lovable scamp, Hermes! Do not miss!

TYPHON

THE LAST SON OF MOTHER EARTH

MONSTER OF	The personification of hurricanes
SACRED ANIMALS	In a way, many, as he sported the heads of one hundred different animals
SACRED PLACE	Mount Etna, Sicily (his final resting place)
HEAVENLY BODY	42355 Typhon, a minor planet
MODERN LEGACY	"Typhoon" is the name for a Pacific Ocean cyclone.

To Mrs. Grace Stamile, in whose classroom I was first introduced to the wonders of Greek mythology.

And to Bronte, Spike, and Zeus. Good boys, all.

—G.O.

New York
A NEAL PORTER BOOK

Published by First Second
First Second is an imprint of Roaring Brook Press,
a division of Holtzbrinck Publishing Holdings Limited Partnership
175 Fifth Avenue, New York, New York 10010

Library of Congress Control Number: 2017941162

Paperback ISBN: 978-1-62672-525-6
Hardcover ISBN: 978-1-62672-524-9

First American edition, 2018

Book design by Rob Steen

Printed in China by Toppan Leefung Printing Ltd., Dongguan City, Guangdong Province

Paperback: 10 9 8 7 6 5 4 3 2 1
Hardcover: 10 9 8 7 6 5 4 3 2 1